Here You Are, Baby

wishes for your
little one

Written by Miriam Hathaway • Illustrated by Jill Labieniec

Here you are baby,

What will you be?

A bundle, a gift,
A hopeful wish,

With tiny hands to hold.

A song, a star,

A brave explorer

With wild stories told.

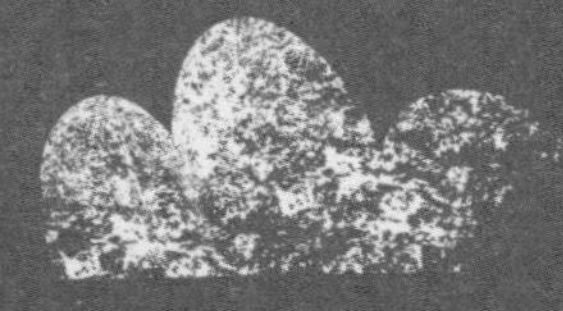

Here you are baby,

What will you have?

Costumes and kisses,

Strength and joy,

And hopes of dreams come true.

Kindness and games,

Wheels and scrapes,

And arms to run into.

Here you are baby,

What will you know?

Secrets, surprises,

Messes and mud,

And peace under a tree.

A snuggle, a dance,
A tickle, a rhyme,
And daring to be free.

Here you are baby,

What will you find?

Mischief and treasure,

Magic and wonder,

And room for you to grow.

Your knees, your toes,
And true delight,
With purpose all your own.

Here you are baby,

What will you do?

March and cheer,

Blossom and bounce,

Clap and reach and play.

Giggle and shine,

Nestle and smile,

And feel loved every day.

With special thanks to the entire Compendium family.

CREDITS:
Written by: Miriam Hathaway
Designed and Illustrated by: Jill Labieniec
Edited by: Ruth Austin

Library of Congress Control Number: 2016910265
ISBN: 978-1-943200-15-3

1st printing. Printed in China with soy inks. A051610001